Norbett's Bistro

PAUL CARSON

About the Author

Paul Carson is a practising medical doctor who lives in Dublin with his wife and two children. He is the author of four other books on health problems in children. *Norbett's Bistro* is his second book for children. *Norbett Bear, MD* was published in 1994.

Norbett's Bistro

PAUL CARSON

POOLBEG

Published in 1995 by
Poolbeg Press Ltd,
Knocksedan House,
123 Baldoyle Industrial Estate,
Dublin 13, Ireland

A catalogue record for this book is available from the British Library.

ISBN 1 85371 462 3

Illustration by Donald Teskey
Cover design by Poolbeg Group Services Ltd
Set by Poolbeg Group Services Ltd in Stone 13/18
Printed by The Guernsey Press Ltd,
Vale, Guernsey, Channel Islands

To Jean, Emily and David yet again

Norbett and Bamber Bears would like especially to thank Emily for her cure for Scuttle, the kangaroo who had lost his hop

Contents

1

Monsieur Norbett Ze Bear, Ze Famous French Chef

Norbett Bear stood admiring himself in the long mirror at the back of his cave. In his right paw he held a book, *French Phrase Book for Bears*.

"'Allo, 'allo," he said to himself in his best French accent. "You are ze very handsome bear. A bear of *magnifique* distinction." He turned sideways and glanced down at the book again. "*Bonjour monsieur* ze bear. 'Ave you been ze long in Paris?" He turned right around and looked at himself from the other side.

"*Non, monsieur*. I am only in ze Paris zis

very . . . zis very . . . zis very *evening*, or, as you ze say in French, zis very *soir*."

He turned straight to the mirror again and held out a paw to himself and pretended to shake his reflection. "*Bonjour*, Norbett ze bear. I 'ave heard so much about you. Pleeze let me ze shake your paw."

"*Certainement*," he said back to himself and bowed to the mirror. Then he threw his head back and let out a hearty laugh. "Attaboy, Norbett Bear. It won't take you long to speak fluent French !"

He put down the book and picked up another which lay on the table in the middle of the cave. *French Cooking Made Easy For Bears* was the title, and Norbett sat down and began to study it closely. He licked the tip of a claw and turned the pages slowly, admiring the photographs of the exotic French dishes displayed. Every now and then he paused to scribble a note on one of the pages. Finally he stood up, stretched himself and walked back to the

Norbett Bear stood admiring himself in the long mirror at the back of the cave

mirror again. "Allo, Norbett ze bear, ze famous French chef. 'Ow are you zis day? I 'ave come to dine at your famous French *bistro.*" He reached into a drawer and pulled out a false moustache, fixing it firmly on his upper lip. It was a long thin moustache, waxed fully so that it curled up at the ends. Norbett inspected the result in the mirror. Then he opened a press and took out a chef's hat and white coat and put them on. He turned right around so that he could see the back of his coat and the writing he had placed there earlier:

Monsieur Norbett ze Bear,
Famous French Chef

Norbett smiled when he saw the final result. "*Monsieur* Norbett," he said to the mirror, "it is ze time to show thees to your faithful first assistant, Bamber ze bear."

He peeled off the moustache and slipped out of his white coat. Very gently he folded the chef's hat and then placed the lot in a bag. "Look out, Bamber ze bear," he shouted to nobody in particular,

"I am ze coming to tell you of my new plans!" He gave a hearty laugh and walked to the cave door, opened it and stuck a notice on the front:

Dr Norbett Bear, MD
Afternoon off today.
If you need a doctor you can call the wizard in the next valley (even though he's pretty useless and I wouldn't let a dog near him).
I have gone to visit my faithful first assistant, Bamber Bear,
and we will be back on duty tomorrow.
If I were you I'd stay well until then.

He picked up his bag and was about to close the door after him when a voice came from behind some bushes. "G'day, sport. You don't happen to know where Dr Norbett bear lives around here, do you?" Into the clearing in front of the cave bounded a kangaroo, followed slowly by another, only this one had his head hung low and seemed to be dragging himself along.

"I am Dr Norbett Bear," replied Norbett haughtily, "with an 'MD' to you."

"And an MD to you too, sport," laughed the kangaroo. "Boy, am I glad to see you. My name's Hoppy. Me and me mate, Scuttle, have travelled miles to see you. Hey, Scuttle," shouted the kangaroo to his mate, "it's that bear we read about."

Norbett put his bag down and inspected the kangaroos closely. "Where have you two come from?"

"Sydney," said Hoppy.

"Sydney who?" asked Norbett.

The kangaroos exchanged puzzled glances. "Wadayou mean, 'Sydney who,' sport?" said Hoppy. "It's Sydney, Australia."

Norbett shook his head. "Sydney Australia. Never heard of him. He's not from around these parts, anyway. Did he send you here?"

The kangaroos exchanged puzzled glances again. Hoppy reached into his pouch and took out a piece of folded-up newspaper and looked at it carefully. He looked again at Norbett. "Excuse me, sport, but are you the famous doctor bear we read about back home? The one who can cure almost anything?"

"Who said *almost* anything?" sniffed Norbett proudly. "Stay where you are."

He marched back inside his cave and returned carrying the sign that stands outside the entrance most days when he and his faithful first assistant, Bamber Bear, are performing their doctoring duties. "Read that," he said to the kangaroos.

Hoppy hopped over and read out loud for the benefit of his friend:

"Forest Medical Centre; Medical Director Dr Norbett Bear, MD; First Assistant Bamber Bear, FA; pains eased, aches relieved, sickness cured. No job too small. Commissions taken. Don't delay, make an appointment today."

When he finished reading Hoppy let out a whoop of delight. "It's him, Scuttle. It's really him. The bear we read about."

He hopped over to Norbett and shook his paw warmly. "Boy, are we glad to see you. We've been travelling for days looking for this place." He suddenly looked worried.

"It's me mate, Scuttle, wot really needs to see you. You see, he's lost his hop. Can't hop anywhere. Scuttles about the place all the time trying to hop but just can't perform yer actual hop. Now I can tell you, bear, that's not much fun for a kangaroo. He's the laughing stock of the Nullabor Plain. Every time the other kangaroos see him coming they all start to put on these enormous big hops just to make him look stupid. Poor old Scuttle just scuttles about the place trying hard not to make himself seen. That's why he's called Scuttle; he just scuttles. Doesn't hop, just scuttles all about the place."

Norbett looked over at Scuttle but he just stood at the edge of the clearing with his head held low, scuffing at the ground with one of his feet. He reached into his pouch, pulled out a handkerchief and blew his nose loudly. Then he wiped a few tears away from his eyes.

Hoppy hopped over and put an arm around his shoulders. "Don't start crying, me old mate," he said. "We've finally tracked down this real famous doctor bear here and I'm sure he'll be able to sort you out." He turned to Norbett. "Won't you, bear?"

Norbett put on his Intelligent Looking Face and then followed it up with his I Care For Sick Animals Face. Then he smiled a warm, reassuring smile at Scuttle. Scuttle smiled weakly back.

"I see no particular great problem here," Norbett announced grandly. "Nothing that we don't handle most days in the medical centre."

"Streuth, that's great," said Hoppy and he gave an enormous hop of delight into the air.

"However," interrupted Norbett, a paw in the air for effect, "I only work with my faithful first assistant, Bamber Bear, who is not actually with me today. It is he who makes up our special medicinal potions. I will have to go and discuss this delicate case with him."

"No worries," said Hoppy. "We've waited this long and we can wait a little longer."

"However," continued Norbett, "until we make up a special hoppity potion for Scuttle, perhaps he should get into practice for some real hopping again. Wait here." Norbett disappeared into the cave and returned a short time later.

"Here," he said to Scuttle, handing him an unusual-looking stick, "start working on this."

Scuttle inspected the stick closely, turning it upside down and from side to side.

"What is it, mate?" he asked.

"A pogo stick," said Norbett.

"A pogo stick!" exclaimed Scuttle and Hoppy together. "What's a pogo stick?"

So Norbett pointed out the features of

the pogo stick and even did a few hops himself to show Scuttle how it worked. Then Scuttle very gingerly got up on the pogo stick himself and began hopping around the clearing.

Norbett placed both paws behind his red braces and snapped them against his chest. He turned to Hoppy. "Well, what do you think so far? He isn't exactly hopping on his own but at least he knows what it's like to hop."

Hoppy was looking intently at Scuttle and noting his every movement. "Do you know, bear, there could be a big market for pogo sticks where I come from."

Norbett gave him a long hard look. "Oh really?" he said.

"No worries, mate," continued Hoppy, all the time watching Scuttle hop this way and that around the clearing. "There's a lot of the older kangaroos who get a bit tired hopping about the place and wouldn't mind having one of yer . . . yer . . . wadidyou call it again?"

"Pogo stick."

"Exactly. Yer actual pogo stick. I might take a few back with me to Sydney."

"Why, can't he hop either?"

Hoppy gave Norbett a strange look. "Can't who hop either?"

"Sydney Australia," said Norbett helpfully.

"Look," said Hoppy, becoming a bit exasperated by now, "Sydney's not a bloke. It's a place in Australia where me and Scuttle come from."

"Oh," said Norbett, trying to look knowledgable and as if he really knew this all the time. "Australia. That's where you two actually come from?"

"Exactly," said Hoppy and he hopped over to where Scuttle had finally settled for a rest. "How's it goin', mate?"

Scuttle's face was smile from corner to corner. He took the handkerchief out from his pouch and wiped his brow. "Brilliant, mate. Just brilliant."

"Sorry to interrupt," said Norbett, "but I was just going over to visit my faithful first assistant, Bamber Bear. You two hang on here for a while and we'll be back a little later."

So Dr Norbett Bear, MD picked up his medical bag, closed the cave door and set off through the forest to visit his one and only first assistant, Bamber Bear.

2

Bamber Ze Bear, Ze Famous Head Waiter

Inside his cave Bamber Bear was having an argument with his weighing scales. "You're wrong," he growled as he inspected the dial. Bamber had been on a diet for a whole week and, to his dismay, found he had put on weight instead of losing it. He jumped up and down on the scales, watching the pointer move back and forward. "You're wrong," he growled again, finally giving the scales a kick. "I'll show you who's boss around here," he shouted, opening his big food press and pulling out a tin of chocolate biscuits. "You can't fool Bamber Bear, first assistant to the world-

famous Dr Norbett Bear, MD." He sat down on a chair at the table in the middle of the cave muttering to himself, picked up a book which lay there and began flicking through the pages. *The Slim-Fast Cookbook for Bears: Lose 100 lbs in One Week.* It was Bamber's favourite book. Every time he read it he felt hungry and every time he read it he just had to have one of his favourite chocolate biscuits. He selected one and inspected it lovingly before popping it straight into his mouth. Licking a few crumbs from his claws he settled back to the chapter he enjoyed reading most: "Eat all you want and still lose weight!"

"I just love this book," he growled as he munched. "'Chapter 3: Who Said Cookies Are Fattening? Eat All You Want And Still Lose Weight!'"

BANG! BANG! BANG! Someone knocked at his cave door.

"Bamber Bear. Are you in there? Open up. It's me." It was Norbett Bear.

Bamber groaned.

BANG! BANG! BANG! "Come on, Bamber. Open up. I have something very important to tell you."

Bamber groaned even more. This could only mean trouble.

The letterbox on his door flipped open and Norbett peered inside. "Are you eating again?" he growled, watching Bamber trying to hide the biscuit tin. "Is it any wonder you can't fit into your special uniform."

Bamber pulled an unpleasant face behind a paw and padded over to the door.

"It's supposed to be our day off," he complained as he pulled at the bolt and finally swung the door open. "We agreed last week. Today was our day off."

Ignoring Bamber's complaints, Norbett strode past him into the cave. He placed both paws behind his red braces and snapped them against his chest. "Bamber Bear," he announced grandly, "I have another GREAT IDEA to discuss with you."

Bamber groaned loudly. Norbett's great ideas usually spelled trouble for him and he was so enjoying his day off from work at the forest Medical Centre where he and Norbett ministered to sick and injured animals.

Norbett held up a paw to silence Bamber's groans. "Bamber Bear. This GREAT IDEA is an even better idea than my last GREAT IDEA which was a BRILLIANT IDEA!"

Bamber looked at him warily. "Oh, yeah. What's this all about, then?"

"Food," said Norbett.

Bamber's face lit up. "Food?" he asked hopefully.

"Indeed, food," said Norbett, picking up a biscuit crumb on the end of a claw and nibbling on it. "Your favourite pastime. Food."

"I like it already," said Bamber. "I'm beginning to like this great idea very much. Tell me more."

Norbett snapped his braces against his chest and put on his Important Announcement Face. He held up a paw for greater effect. Bamber listened attentively.

"Bamber Bear," began Norbett, "you and I. Me and you. Us two. The two of us. Both of us. Together . . . "

"Oh get on with it," snapped Bamber. "I haven't got all day to wait for this. What is this great idea?"

Norbett opened the bag he had brought with him, bent down and began rummaging through it. He had his back to Bamber. Finally he stood up and turned around.

"What's that under your nose?" said Bamber, squinting at Norbett's moustache. "A hamster?"

"'Allo, 'allo, Bamber ze bear. 'Ow do you do? I am so pleezed to be making your acquaintance? Pleeze let me shake your paw."

Bamber's mouth opened and closed but nothing came out.

Norbett reached inside the bag again and quickly donned his chef's coat.

Then ever so slowly he placed the chef's hat on his head.

Bamber's mouth opened and stayed open. He gulped and then gulped again.

Then he gulped once more. "What . . . what . . . who . . . who . . . what . . . who . . . what?"

Norbett marched around the cave, twirling the ends of his moustache and speaking in his best French accent. "Bamber ze bear," he announced, "you are now looking at Norbett ze bear, ze famous French chef from Paris. Forget about all ze rubbishy food you have ever eaten before in your bear-type life, I will bring a new style of cooking to zis forest zat ze animals have never experienced before. You and I," here he paused and looked directly at Bamber who still stood with his mouth wide open, "you and I, Bamber ze bear, will open *Norbett's Bistro*, a very posh French restaurant in this 'ere forest. What do you zink of zat, Bamber ze bear, and pleeze close that mouth of yours before ze flies make zer homes in it!"

Bamber snapped his mouth shut and put on his Hurt Face. "What do you know about French cooking?" he asked, pouting.

"Nothing, nothing at all, *mon petit* Bamber. But I 'ave been ze reading all about it and zere is nothing to it at all. You just have to dress like a French chef, speak in ze mock posh French accent – just like I am ze doing at theese moment – and ze animals around ze forest will flock to us."

"Oh," said Bamber, pretending he understood all this perfectly, but really his head was spinning.

"Do you like my special French chef's uniform?" asked Norbett, turning right around so that Bamber could see the writing on the back.

"Oh, very good," enthused Bamber admiringly.

"And I 'ave one for you too, *mon petit* Bamber ze bear. I 'ave a special uniform for you as well."

Now if there is one thing Bamber Bear really likes about Norbett Bear's grand plans, it is that they always involve special uniforms. When he first assists at the Forest Medical Centre Bamber always wears his special yellow assistant's coat with his name written on the back: *Bamber Bear, First Assistant to Dr Norbett Bear, MD*. Indeed, Bamber is so fond of his uniform that he often forgets to take it off at night and ends up sleeping in it. Norbett is forever telling him off for turning up to first assist with his uniform all creased and crumpled.

"Special uniform," whispered Bamber, "special uniform. What special uniform? I just love special uniforms. Show me my special uniform."

So Norbett reached into the bag again and produced a pair of pin-striped trousers which Bamber slipped into immediately. Next he produced a starched white shirt and black bow-tie. Finally, after Bamber had put these on, Norbett pulled out a long black jacket from the bag and slipped it over Bamber's shoulders. Bamber rushed over to the mirror at the back of the cave and inspected the result. He looked very impressive.

"One moment," said Norbett, "I almost forgot this." He stood behind Bamber as he looked in the mirror and placed a long, black waxed moustache on his upper lip. Norbett licked his claws and curled the moustache up at the ends. "Now turn around, *mon petit* Bamber ze bear, and let me see what is written on the back of your jacket."

So Bamber turned around slowly and read the writing on the back of his new jacket out loud:

Bamber ze bear
Posh French Head Waiter
Orders Taken: Do Not Open
Your Mouth Until Asked

"Oh, nice one," murmured Bamber, delighted with his outfit. "'Bamber bear, Posh French Head Waiter.' I like that. I could live with that."

"Attaboy, Bamber," said Norbett. "You look really smart in this outfit."

Bamber stood admiring himself in the mirror for some time, turning this way and that to see how he looked. Suddenly he turned to Norbett. "Why can't I be the chef and you be the head waiter. Huh?"

"Because, Bamber *mon petit*, you are ze bear with ze magnifique appetite. You spend all day eating, or thinking of eating, or dreaming you are eating. If I put you in charge of ze cooking you might be your own best customer. Barely would ze food be cooked than down ze hatch it would go into Bamber ze bear's own tummy."

Bamber started to protest but Norbett waved a paw at him and shook his head. "Non, *mon petit* Bamber ze bear. I am ze head chef, you will be ze famous posh French head waiter. You will take ze orders from ze forest animals and convey ze same orders to me, Monsieur Norbett ze bear, ze famous French chef, where they will then be cooked to perfection."

Bamber inspected himself in the mirror again, delighted with how smart he looked. He wet the tip of his claws and twisted at the ends of the wax moustache so that it looked even more curly than Norbett's. Then he turned sideways, pulling his tummy in for better effect. "I like it," he murmured, "I like this special uniform very much."

"You look very smart," said Norbett,

flicking a piece of fur off Bamber's shoulder. "And once you have learned a bit of French there'll be no stopping you."

"French!" gasped Bamber. "I have to speak French? I know nothing about French."

"Do not worry your bear-type little head," said Norbett soothingly, "there will be an intensive training course before we open ze famous *Norbett's Bistro.*"

"Oh no," groaned Bamber, holding his head in both paws. "Not training exercises. I hate your training exercises."

Norbett placed a comforting paw around his shoulder. "Do not worry, *mon petit,* these will be ze very simple training exercises. Just a few phrases to be going along with."

Norbett sat Bamber down at the table in the middle of the cave. He marched around the table, twirling at the ends of his waxed moustache. "First of all, Bamber ze bear, you must speak with ze posh French accent."

Bamber groaned.

"*Pardonement*, Bamber, did I hear ze groan escape from you?"

Bamber pulled a face behind a paw.

"Now," continued Norbett, "let us begin. You must a speak like zis in your best type posh French accent." Norbett then plucked a handkerchief from inside his chef's uniform and lay it across his left arm.

"Always carry zis cloth like zis when you are serving ze customers."

"Why?" asked Bamber, his head spinning.

"Because ze customers are usually a bunch of ze messiest eaters you are ever likely to come across in your bear-type life and you will need ze cloth to flick ze crumbs from ze table."

"Oh," said Bamber, trying to brush away the biscuit crumbs he had left on the table without Norbett noticing.

"And remember zis, ze most important tip of all in our new bistro: *ze customer is always wrong.*"

Bamber's mouth opened and closed. "The customer is always wrong?"

"Not 'the' customer, 'ze' customer, if you pleeze, Bamber, *mon petit,*" corrected Norbett. "*Exactement.* You can take whatever ze order ze customer asks for but you give him back whatever *I* zink he deserves."

Bamber started to say something but was so addled he forget what he was going to say and just sat there, slightly dazed.

"Now," continued Norbett, "you can read ze book from which I 'ave learned all my best French. But first we must return to ze Medical Centre to recover my pogo stick."

By this stage Bamber's head was so confused he just couldn't figure out one thing Norbett was saying.

"Pogo stick?" he muttered, shaking his head from side to side. "Pogo stick?"

"Ah, yes," interrupted Norbett. "I forgot to mention that bit to you. I know it's your day off but we have a couple of kangaroos back at the Medical Centre looking for help. I told them we would be back soon to see how to help one of them find his hop again."

Bamber said nothing for a moment, his eyes glazed, his head reeling. "Norbett," he finally said slowly, "Norbett . . . "

"*Oui, mon petit* Bamber ze bear."

"Norbett," continued Bamber, his brain desperately trying to take in all this new information. "Norbett. If we continue doctoring at the Medical Centre, when are we going to work at this posh new French restaurant?"

"In the evening, Bamber *mon petit*, in the evening whenever the Medical Centre has closed for the day." Norbett placed a comforting paw on Bamber's shoulder. "We take down our Medical Centre sign and put up our new sign: *Norbett's Bistro*, Posh French Restaurant. All this will take place in the evening. What do you think of that, *mon petit* Bamber?"

"Aaaaggggghhhh!" roared Bamber. "Aaaagggghh!"

3

Norbett's Bistro

When Norbett and Bamber returned to Norbett's cave there was no sign of the two kangaroos. Norbett took in the Medical Centre sign and placed the new sign he had painted carefully the day before in front of the door:

Norbett's Bistro
Posh French Restuarant
Opening Soon

"Now, Bamber," said Norbett, "we'll slip into our new uniforms and have a few training exercises while we wait for our first customers."

"Righto," agreed Bamber, only too delighted to look impressive in his pin-striped trousers, white shirt, bow tie and long black jacket. He stuck his new waxed moustache on to his upper lip and paraded around the cave talking to imaginary customers in his best mock French accent.

"Ah, *monsieur* ze 'orse, 'ow are you zis night? You have come for a little light snack perhaps? Do ze sit down in ze far corner where I 'ave reserved ze best table for you."

"Attaboy, Bamber," enthused Norbett as he looked on. "Attaboy. Don't forget to show him the menu."

"*Mais certainement, monsieur* Norbett ze bear, *certainement*. One moment if you pleeze," said Bamber, pretending to search for the menu. "We haven't got a menu."

"A good point, *mon petit* Bamber, a good point," mused Norbett, looking around the cave. "And we haven't set any tables for our victims . . . sorry, I should have

said customers." He chuckled behind a paw.

So Norbett and Bamber pulled out their one and only table into the middle of the cave and set two chairs on either side of it.

"A checked tablecloth, perhaps?" asked Bamber and Norbett nodded his approval.

"We'd better put a few knives and forks down too," added Norbett and there then began an argument as to where exactly the cutlery should go. Bamber wanted it one way, but Norbett insisted on another. Bamber pulled himself up to his full height, twirled at the ends of his moustache and announced grandly, "If I am to be the head waiter in this posh establishment then I should have final say over where the knives and forks go. You," and here he pointed to the kitchen, "are in charge of the cooking, while I am in charge of the floor."

Norbett mumbled something behind his moustache and retired to the back of the cave and his pots and pans. Bamber set about preparing the table, first laying a checked cloth across it, followed by the knives, forks and spoons in the exact order he wanted. Then, with a grand French flourish, he stuck a few flowers into a glass of water and placed it firmly in the centre of the table.

"Well, what do you think?" he addressed the scowling Norbett who was shining one of his pans for the tenth time as he looked on.

Suddenly there came a knock on the cave door. Norbett and Bamber exchanged glances. "I'm not really ready yet for any customers," hissed Bamber.

"Nor am I," whispered Norbett, "but we have to start somewhere. Open the door and let's see how we get on."

"But what about a menu?" Bamber hissed again.

"You deal with whoever it is at the door and I'll scribble something quickly," Norbett whispered back.

The door was knocked on again and Bamber pulled it open with a grand flourish.

"*Bonjour, monsieur*. Welcome to *Norbett's Bistro*, ze very famous and posh French restaurant."

There, standing outside the cave door, stood a fox, the very same fox Norbett and Bamber had nearly knocked unconscious some weeks earlier when they had been pretending to be ambulances. The unfortunate fox had got caught up in one of their training exercises and was knocked almost into oblivion. Indeed, so shaken was he by the whole event, he had difficulty remembering things ever since. Even Norbett's special memory medicine had failed to restore him to his full senses.

Bamber looked at the fox and the fox looked at Bamber. The fox closed his eyes very slowly and very tightly and then very, very slowly opened them again.

"'Allo, 'allo, *monsieur* Reynard ze fox. You are looking very well and . . . how you say? very hungry as well. 'Ave you come to eat at our famous and posh French restaurant?"

The fox closed his eyes again, shuddered and shook his head violently as if trying to dislodge some troublesome image. Then he opened his eyes again, one at a time.

Bamber beamed a smile past his waxed moustache. "'Allo, 'allo again, *monsieur* Reynard ze fox. You seem slightly addled in your fox-type brain. Welcome again to *Norbett's Bistro*, the new posh French restaurant just opened zis very day."

From inside the cave Bamber heard Norbett give a muffled cheer. "Great, Bamber. Absolutely great!"

"Who are you?" asked the fox finally, half afraid of what the answer might be.

"I am Bamber ze bear, ze famous head waiter in this 'ere very famous French restaurant."

"Bamber ze bear?" repeated the fox, bemused and confused by the vision of Bamber in his new head waiter's uniform.

"*Exactement, monsieur* Reynard ze fox. Bamber ze bear, ze head waiter."

"You're really Bamber Bear, the first assistant to Dr Norbett Bear, aren't you?" laughed the fox weakly. "I mean, you're really just Bamber Bear. Aren't you? The Bamber Bear I know?"

Bamber sniffed and looked down past his moustache at the fox. *"Non!"* he said emphatically. "You are mistaken, *monsieur*

Reynard ze fox. I am Bamber ze bear, ze twin brother of the other Bamber bear that you seem to know so much about."

"Brilliant!" shouted Norbett from inside, but just loud enough for Bamber's ears.

The fox shook his head again, as if in a daze. "His twin brother?"

"*Exactement.* His twin brother from France."

"From France," muttered the fox, beginning to feel faint and breaking out in a cold sweat. He knew he hadn't been feeling all that well since his accident when he was knocked senseless in the middle of the forest by Bamber and Norbett. He had been having terrible lapses of memory and kept turning up at the Medical Centre for more of Dr Norbett's memory medicine. He just knew he wasn't feeling his normal self but at this precise moment he was having more than his usual difficulty with what he was seeing and hearing.

"His twin brother from France?" the fox repeated.

"Exactement," replied Bamber grandly. "And believe it or not, *monsieur* Reynard ze fox, guess whose twin brother also came with me?"

The fox's eyes began to spin in his head and he grinned a stupid grin at Bamber. "You mean there's more than one of you in there?"

Suddenly Norbett appeared at Bamber's side, fully dressed in his chef's outfit. "*Bonjour, monsieur* Reynard ze fox. And ze jolly good day to you and 'ow are you this fine day in your fox-type life?"

The fox's eyes glazed over and his mouth began to tremble. He looked from one bear to the other and then back to the first bear again. His hind legs began to feel weak and he sat down for support. "Who . . . who . . . who . . . no, don't tell me, don't tell me!" he groaned. "Don't tell me. I suppose you're Norbett Bear's twin brother?"

"Quel génie," growled Norbett in mock surprise. "What a genius! *Magnifique, monsieur* Reynard ze fox, you are truly ze genius. 'Ow did you know who I am?"

The fox began to giggle slightly hysterically and wiped a tear away from his eye with a shaky paw. "I'm just not well," he muttered to himself. "I'm just not a well fox. I haven't been well since that accident. But I thought I was recovering, I really did." He paused and looked up again at Norbett and Bamber who smiled down at him past their waxed moustaches. He shook his head sadly again. "I'm just not a well fox, that's all there is to it."

"Nonsense," interrupted Norbett and he reached down and took the fox's front paw in his own. "You are just a 'ungry fox. You look as if you 'ave not eaten a decent meal for some time. Why don't you come into our posh French restaurant and 'ave a bite to eat. Then you will feel much better."

Half whimpering, half shuddering, mostly looking as if he had lost his marbles, the fox was gently led inside by Bamber and Norbett and sat down at the table in the middle of the cave. Bamber made a great show of brushing the table around him and humming to himself. Norbett handed him a menu and then disappeared to the back of the cave and began banging a few pots and pans together to make the right restaurant noises he had read about. The fox looked around the cave fearfully, as if some more weird characters might suddenly appear at any moment.

Finally Bamber stood beside the fox, white cloth draped over one arm. "Are you ready to order, monsieur Reynard?"

The fox looked up at Bamber and licked his lips hungrily. He bared his sharp teeth and snapped them together a few times. "Yes," he said, his confidence coming back. "I think I'll have chicken. Yes, that would do nicely. I'll have chicken."

"Certainement," murmured Bamber, making a great show of writing all this down on a piece of paper. "And 'ow would *monsieur* like his chicken?"

"Squawking!" cried the fox, raking his claws across the table in front of him. "Squawking! Just let him loose and let him run around the place a bit so I can work up a real appetite just watching him and then just let me chase him a bit around the table." The fox was getting quite agitated by now and began drooling at the mouth. Even Bamber looked a bit taken aback. "And then, just when he's getting tired, I'll sneak up behind . . . "

Bamber held up a paw for silence. "*Monsieur* Reynard ze fox," he announced solemnly, "zis is ze posh French restaurant, not a chicken roost in some farmer's yard. Ze food is served on ze table in front of you. It is not usual to chase it all around ze place before you eat it!"

At this point Norbett appeared at Bamber's side. "*Excusement,* Bamber ze bear, ze head waiter. Are you having some difficulty with zis customer?"

Bamber started to explain all about the fox's request for his chicken to be served squawking and let loose around the cave so that the fox could have a real chase before finally catching it. Norbett stood listening, a pot held in one paw. Unfortunately at this point Bamber's waxed moustache started to come loose and began peeling away from his upper lip. Norbett looked on aghast, trying desperately to catch Bamber's attention with a wave of his free paw. The fox stared in total fascination as the moustache became looser and looser. "You're not Bamber ze bear at all," he interrupted in amazement, "you're just plain old Bamber Bear, FA . . . "

BANG! BOING! BANG! BOING! Norbett suddenly crashed the pot against the table. BANG! BOING! BANG! He did it again and the fox took an almighty leap into the air in fright.

"So sorry," roared Norbett at the top of his voice, "I thought I saw a horrible big bluebottle fly on ze table and I tried to squash it!" With his free paw he quickly stretched across and stuck Bamber's moustache back on.

The fox's nerves were totally shattered by now and he began to whimper again, staring at the cave door longingly, desperate for an escape from these two mad bears. His paws began to shake and his teeth started chattering.

"Perhaps," suggested Norbett

soothingly as he placed a comforting paw around the fox's shoulder, "perhaps you need to see ze doctor bear and his faithful first assistant? You look a little . . . 'ow you say . . . shaken."

"Oh, yes please," pleaded the fox. "Maybe you could get hold of your twin brothers for me? They have such marvellous medicines. I'm sure they could brew up something for me. I feel so strange and addled."

"Certainement," said Bamber. "Wait here, my fox-type friend, and I will seek out my brother zis very moment."

The fox sat nervously at the table, barely daring to speak, smiling weakly at Norbett who bustled around the cave pretending to tidy up the place.

Bamber slipped out the back and quickly cast off his head waiter uniform, returning moments later in his famous first assistant outfit.

"Ah, fox!" he exclaimed in mock

surprise. "Back again, I see. Looking for some more memory medicine, perhaps?"

"Bamber Bear," whimpered the fox with relief, "am I glad to see you! I'm just after meeting some nut who told me he was your twin brother."

"Ah," said Bamber, knowingly, "you mean Bamber ze bear from Australia?"

"Australia!" whimpered the fox, his head reeling again. "He said he was from France."

"Same place," replied Bamber, slightly flustered. "It's just down the road from the real France. You turn left at Russia, take a right past Germany, jump over the bridge between Chile and Austria, climb over the fence that separates England from China and there you are. Australia, southern France."

"Oh," said the fox. "So that's where he came from." He giggled nervously.

"Exactly," said Bamber grandly. "You know, I haven't seen him for years, and when he and Norbett Bear's twin brother turned up unexpectedly we were delighted to see them again."

"Were you?" whimpered the fox, looking over his shoulder at Norbett who still stood nearby in his chef's outfit, smiling broadly past his waxed moustache.

"Really delighted," continued Bamber, "and do you know what?"

"What?" asked the fox, not sure he really wanted to hear the reply.

"They are going to open a posh French restaurant right here in this very cave."

The fox looked around the cave, his head spinning again, his eyes rolling in his head. "But what about the Medical Centre?"

"Ze world-famous Medical Centre run by my twin brother Dr Norbett Bear, MD," interrupted Norbett in his best posh French accent, "will continue in zis very cave during ze day and by night ze very posh and famous French restaurant will open for ze business. It will serve only ze poshest and most famous of ze French food."

"Bamber," pleaded the fox, now so addled and distracted by all the strange goings-on that he could barely think straight, "Bamber, have you anything in your medicine chest for a fox whose nerves are totally shattered?"

"You mean our special 'Lost The Marbles, Gone Totally Bananas medicine'?"

"Oh yes, please," said the fox eagerly, "that sounds just the stuff for me."

So while Norbett stood by, a grin fixed behind his false moustache, Bamber went to the back of the cave and returned moments later with a green bottle containing a foul-smelling yellow mixture. The fox snatched it from his paws and almost knocked the whole bottle back in one go. He pulled a most unpleasant face before sticking the cork back on again. "I feel better already," he giggled nervously and slowly made for the door, all the time keeping a wary eye on Norbett whose jaws were beginning to ache from keeping his stupid-looking grin in place.

"Good luck with the restaurant," shouted the fox at the cave door as he turned on his hind legs and bolted into the safety of the forest.

Norbett and Bamber closed the door and sat down at the table in the middle of the cave. Bamber looked at Norbett and Norbett looked at Bamber. The waxed moustache on Norbett's upper lip was now also slowly peeling away and beginning to droop downwards. Norbett tried to blow it back up, but every time he blew he managed only to dislodge it further.

"'Allo, Norbett ze bear, ze famous French chef," giggled Bamber, "you look silly!"

Even Norbett could contain himself no longer and started to laugh and laugh. "I think," he spluttered, "we may 'ave to buy some stronger glue for our moustaches before we open the doors of our restaurant again!"

Bamber said nothing; he was lying on the floor in the middle of the cave, holding his sides with both paws, convulsed with laughter.

4

Some Strange Treatments

The next day Norbett and Bamber decided to open the First Forest Medical Centre as usual. "We'll have to get in some more practice at the *Bistro*," suggested Norbett, "before we put out that sign again."

"OK," agreed Bamber unhappily. He thought he looked so well in his new uniform, he much preferred wearing it to the usual yellow coat he wore around the Medical Centre. Still, he had to agree neither he nor Norbett really knew what they were doing at the *Bistro*. They needed more practice at being posh French chefs and even posher French head waiters.

When Bamber finally opened the cave doors, there was a long queue of sick and injured animals waiting to see them. Indeed, the queue stretched so far back into the forest Bamber could not make out what sort of animals were actually at the very end.

"OK," said Norbett wearily. "Show the first one in."

Into the cave padded a lion. Bamber looked nervously at Norbett but Norbett held up a reassuring paw and told the lion to sit down at the table in the middle of the cave. "What seems to be the matter, Mr Lion?" he asked.

"I've got the hiccups," replied the lion sadly, his face as long as today and tomorrow.

"The hiccups?" interrupted Bamber.

"Yes, bear, the hiccups." The lion shifted uncomfortably in the chair, trying not to look as embarrassed as he felt. "It only comes on when I roar. I'm fine for most of the day but as soon as I start a half-decent

roar out comes this loud hiccup and I can't finish the roar at all. There I am in the middle of the Serengeti, stalking a gazelle or a wildebeest, hungry as anything." The lion paused and looked at Bamber for some sign of sympathetic support.

Bamber gave a feeble smile. This was a big lion and looked pretty fierce to Bamber. He didn't much fancy the idea of being stalked by him in the Serengeti or indeed anywhere else for that matter. "Oh, I understand," he said reassuringly.

"Anyway," continued the lion, "there I am, just about to pounce. The sun's beating down on me, I'm tired and as hungry as can be. But I'm downwind so no animal can smell me coming." At this point the lion suddenly jumped up on the table to demonstrate the hunt. Norbett and Bamber leapt back in surprise. The lion hunched his head low between his shoulders and started a low, deep rumbling growl which seemed to come from inside his stomach.

Bamber began to chew on the ends of his claws nervously. The lion crouched down on all four legs and shook his mane. His eyes narrowed to tiny slits and he looked the most frightening and fearful beast both Norbett and Bamber had ever seen. Even Norbett began to feel a little uneasy and backed away slowly. "Wh . . . wh . . . what happens then?" he stammered.

"Then," growled the lion menacingly, his claws by now dug deep into the table, his hind legs poised to lift him into a leap, "then I bide my time until the gazelle or wildebeest is grazing comfortably, completely unaware of me."

"And then what happens?" stuttered Norbett, backing away.

"Then I pounce!" roared the lion, leaping off the table with an almighty bound right on top of poor Bamber who almost swooned when he saw the huge lumbering beast fly at him through the air. "Roooaaarrr . . . hiccup!" went the lion, astride the now prostrate Bamber. "Rrrroooaaarrr . . . hiccup!" went the lion and he shook his mane angrily.

Bamber couldn't help himself as he stifled a giggle. He hadn't heard anything quite so ridiculous before this – a lion as fierce as the one now standing over him trying desperately to roar but only hiccuping instead.

The lion hung his head in shame. "See what I mean," he complained. "I can get all the stalking right, there's no problem with that. And I can get all the pouncing right, actually catch my prey. No problem with that either. But any decent, self respecting lion who has caught a gazelle or wildebeest wants to let out a good old-fashioned roar at this stage. A roar warns off any other would-be challengers, lets everyone know I've made a successful catch and that supper's on its way back to my lair. How would you feel if just at this important point your prey starts to laugh straight into your face? You're standing astride your gazelle or your wildebeest, all angry and hungry like, trying desperately to let out a real, full-blooded roar but you only end up hiccuping. After a few goes at this, your gazelle or your wildebeest is doubled up with laughter and can hardly lie still for rolling around the ground giggling."

The lion climbed off Bamber, padded back to the chair and sat down wearily. "I can tell you, bear," he said to Norbett sadly, "it has me disgraced where I come from. I'm the laughing stock of the Serengeti plain. Me heart's not in the hunt anymore. I'd almost prefer to go hungry than be laughed at by every animal from antelopes to zebras." Here he became quite agitated. "Hyenas are the worst. They have a horrible laugh at the best of times but whenever they see me coming they just can't control themselves and can be heard all over the plain." His head hung low again in shame. "I'm supposed to be king of the jungle, not the laughing stock of the Serengeti." The lion sniffed and brushed a paw against his snout. "I just hate those mangey hyenas and their horrible laugh. I do, I really do." He looked up again at Norbett who, by now, was back at the table taking notes. "That's when I heard about you and Bamber Bear. The best doctor bears in the world, I heard. So I made my way here to see if you could help. What do you think?" he asked hopefully.

Norbett and Bamber exchanged worried glances. "It's a difficult case, Mr Lion," said Norbett, "but nothing that myself and my faithful first assistant can't handle. We've dealt with bigger problems than this, I can tell you; haven't we, Bamber?"

"Oh, yes," murmured Bamber, trying desperately to remember these other big problems. He put on his Puzzled-Looking Face.

"I'd be so grateful, Dr Norbett," said the lion, stretching a paw across the table and shaking Norbett's paw. "Anything to get my roar back and stop those mangey hyenas from laughing at me."

"Leave it to me, Mr Lion," replied Norbett, showing him out of the cave. "I want you to wait over at the edge of the clearing until Bamber and I think of some way to cure those hiccups."

As the lion padded away Bamber muttered into Norbett's ear: "What are we going to do for this one? He's a fearsome lion; I wouldn't like to get on the wrong side of him, hiccups or no hiccups."

Norbett thought this over carefully. "Usually I'd suggest we creep up behind him and give him an enormous fright. That usually shifts the hiccups in any animal."

Bamber looked aghast. "Gi . . . gi . . . gi . . . give HIM a fright! Give HIM a fright! Have you felt the weight of HIM on top of you? He's not the sort of animal you'd want to frighten!" he protested.

"I know, I know," muttered Norbett thoughtfully. "Leave him over there for a while; I'll think of something. We can't have him coming all the way from the

Serengeti plains and going home telling everybody he couldn't be cured by the famous Dr Norbett Bear and his faithful first assistant."

"Where is the Serengeti anyway?" asked Bamber from behind a paw, trying not to let the lion hear him.

"France," replied Norbett firmly. "Smack bang in the middle of France."

"France?" exclaimed Bamber, puzzled. "I thought it might be somewhere near China."

"No," said Norbett emphatically, "France it is. The place is overrun with lions."

"And gazelles and wildebeest?" asked Bamber, eyebrows raised.

"Knee-deep in them," said Norbett, stroking his chin thoughtfully. "It's an extraordinary place, France is. Full of wildlife and posh French cooks."

"Oh," said Bamber, putting on his Extremely Puzzled-Looking Face.

"Next patient," ordered Norbett and Bamber went to the front of the queue.

There stood a spindle-legged giraffe with the longest face and sorest neck Bamber had ever seen. From just beneath the giraffe's chin and winding all the way along his long neck was an enormous bandage. Bamber stood open-mouthed for a moment. "Is the doctor in?" asked the giraffe. "I'd like to see Dr Norbett Bear MD please," he added. Bamber poked his head back inside the cave and muttered something to Norbett who promptly marched to the front door and looked up. "Sore throat?" he asked.

"No," moaned the giraffe, "I've got a sore neck. In fact I've got a very sore neck. Our local witch doctor says I'm suffering from whiplash. He says it's the sorest thing he's ever seen in his life. That's what he said. He said that a giraffe with a whiplash injury to the neck is the sorest thing in the whole wide world." The giraffe sniffed and lifted one of his spindly front legs to massage his neck. "Do you think you can help?"

There stood a spindle-legged giraffe with the longest face and sorest neck Bamber had ever seen

"Whiplash!" declared Norbett and Bamber together, and they looked at one another in puzzlement. "What's whiplash?"

"Well," began the giraffe, "It all started like this. I was wandering down to our local watering-hole with a few of my mates one very hot day. I was at the front and the other three were directly behind. We were walking in a straight line and then I said 'Let's have a race' and we all started running at the same time, me in front and they following close behind." Norbett and Bamber listened attentively. "Suddenly," continued the giraffe, "an enormous big elephant walked straight in front of me and I had to slam on the brakes to avoid crashing into him." The giraffe stopped and looked down at Norbett and Bamber. Nobody spoke for a moment, then Bamber piped up. "So?" he said.

"So," continued the giraffe mournfully, "I came to a perfect stop but my three mates all crashed into the back of me at the same time. Or rather one after the other. One . . . BANG! Two . . . BANG! Three . . . BANG!" The giraffe winced as he remembered the horrible incident. Again nobody spoke for a moment. Finally Norbett broke the silence. "So?" he said.

"So," snapped the giraffe, "I injured my neck. A giraffe has a very long and delicate neck. A giraffe isn't used to being crashed into from behind by other giraffes, all speeding at the same time. My neck got bounced about in the collision and my local witch doctor says it's called whiplash and he says it's the sorest injury in the world for a giraffe." He paused again. "So there," he added finally. "Can you do anything to help me? My witch doctor says I'm too far gone for him to be of any use. That's why I came to see you."

Norbett and Bamber exchanged glances for a moment and then Norbett addressed the giraffe. "Ahem, no problem as far as I can see, Mr Giraffe. Maybe if you took that bandage from around your neck and let me have a look at it myself, my faithful first assistant and I might be able to decide what treatment you need." Bamber put on his Terribly Important-Looking Face and nodded in agreement with Norbett's every word. So yards of bandage were painfully unwound from around the giraffe's neck. "Just bend your head right down, if you please," asked Norbett and he ran his paws along the giraffe's neck. "Ouch . . . ooh . . . ouch," groaned the giraffe with every touch. Finally Norbett came to an extra and unusually bumpy part of the giraffe's neck and massaged it slowly. His brow furrowed as he felt and he nodded wisely to Bamber who nodded wisely back, putting on his Very Wise Face.

"One moment, please," said Norbett to the giraffe, calling Bamber aside for a discussion. The two bears stood slightly away from the giraffe, muttering to one another. Every now and then Norbett would wave a paw in the air as he explained his plan to Bamber and Bamber waved his paws about as well for effect. He had changed to his Very Thoughtful and Intelligent Face. Finally they returned to the giraffe and Norbett addressed him again.

"Mr Giraffe," he began, "my faithful first assistant and myself and I have worked out a special plan to cure your neck." The giraffe gave a huge sigh of relief and stomped his spindly front legs on the ground with delight. Norbett held up a paw for attention. "However," he continued, "this plan may seem a little strange at first but if you just keep your head down and let us get on with the job then I feel sure you'll go home very much better." The giraffe nodded his head painfully in agreement. "Absolutely, absolutely. Anything at all. Whatever you say."

"Very good," said Norbett and he and Bamber set about their tasks. First of all Bamber disappeared into the cave while

Norbett padded over to the lion who was standing at the edge of the clearing looking on. Norbett told him to stand up straight on all four paws and pointed him so that he was looking in the opposite direction to where the giraffe stood. Then he rushed back to the giraffe. "Head down," he shouted and caught the giraffe by the ears as soon as his long neck wafted them near Norbett's paws.

From inside the cave Bamber Bear rushed out carrying a bucket full of icy water which he quickly strapped to the top of the giraffe's neck. The giraffe had a look of pure astonishment on his face and started to say something but found that Norbett had clamped his mouth shut with both paws. From inside his famous first assistant uniform pocket, Bamber produced a packet which he quickly showed to Norbett who nodded his approval. Written on the side of the packet was **Very Strong Sneezing Powder**. Suddenly Bamber shouted, "Go!" and Norbett released his grasp on the giraffe's mouth while Bamber sprinkled some of the sneezing powder on to his nose. Then Norbett and Bamber both placed their paws around the giraffe's neck and held on for dear life. The giraffe wrinkled his nose slightly, sniffed a little and gave a tiny little sneeze. Then, from deep inside his chest and all the way up his extra long neck a huge sneeze built up. The giraffe tried to stifle it with one of his front hooves but to no avail. As the pressure became too much he felt the itch rush from deep inside and he let out an enormous, loud sneeze. "SNEEZE!" he went, and he tried to lift his head up in the air only to find the weight of the bears holding him down.

"Let go!" roared Norbett and both he and Bamber suddenly released their grip on the giraffe's neck. The giraffe's head shot up into the air like a rocket. Just as quickly, Norbett and Bamber rushed across the clearing towards the lion. Bamber ran to his front and started pulling faces at him. "Roar, Mr Lion," he shouted, "come on and give us one of your roars." At the other side of the clearing the bucket of icy water that had been strapped to the giraffe's neck was now flying through the air, projected by the sudden and dramatic release of the giraffe's head after the enormous sneeze.

"Roar, bear, roar?" said the lion, puzzled, "but I can't roar. That's why I'm here, you great goof." At that split second Norbett caught hold of the lion's tail and gave it an almighty yank. "Roar," began the lion in fury as he turned around to find Norbett Bear also pulling faces at him. "Roar . . . roar . . . hiii . . ." His roar was just about to break into a hiccup when the icy water hit him full in the face.

"ROAR . . . ROAR . . . ROAR!!!" The lion leapt about the clearing like a cat on a hot tin roof, roaring for all he was worth, and never once did a hiccup break through. Suddenly he stopped and stood still, a puzzled look on his face. "Roar,"

he went again, only this time a little more subdued as he tested out his new strength. "Roar?" He could hardly believe his luck and finally he threw back his head and let out an enormous roar that could be heard all over the forest. Not once did he hiccup and he bounded over to Norbett and Bamber delighted with himself. "I've got my roar back," he announced triumphantly, "I've got my roar back."

"And I've lost that dreadful pain in my neck," shouted the giraffe from the other side of the clearing as he gingerly massaged his neck. The sore and tender bumpy lump in the middle had gone, pushed back into place by the enormous sneeze. The giraffe cantered across the clearing and grabbed Norbett by the paw and shook it vigorously. The lion gave Bamber's face a huge lick of delight. Bamber pulled an Unpleasant Face. But all four animals were delighted with themselves, the lion for getting back his roar and the giraffe for getting rid of his sore neck. Norbett and Bamber bears had on their Very Pleased With Ourselves Faces as they watched the lion and giraffe disappear into the forest, to which all the other sick animals in the queue had fled as soon as all the roaring had started.

"Another job well done, even if I say so myself," said Norbett, polishing his claws on his lapels. Bamber wiped his brow and sighed deeply. "I know, I know," he agreed, "but I don't know how we're going to keep up all these hairy, scary cures. I don't know what would have happened to me if that water had missed the lion and he hadn't got his roar back. I was the one in front of him, pulling faces." Norbett grinned widely. "Don't worry, Bamber," he said, "if anything had gone wrong I would have been the first to run for help."

Bamber Bear's mouth opened and closed, but nothing came out.

5

Customers at the *Bistro*

That evening, after a rest, Bamber bear placed the *Bistro* sign outside the cave. There wasn't an animal to be seen anywhere and as the light faded, Bamber could feel a chill in the air. He pulled his tail-coat together at the front and rubbed his paws together for warmth. The moon was just visible behind some clouds and Bamber could see a few stars twinkling in the sky.

Everything was quiet and peaceful. Bamber sighed contentedly. Curing the lion and giraffe had left him tired and he wasn't quite up to Norbett's idea of working nights as well as days. He secretly hoped there wouldn't be any customers. In fact he desperately hoped there wouldn't be any customers, because he had eaten almost all the food in Norbett's larder. If any animal called looking for posh French food they would be in for a big disappointment. Bamber sniffed the air, adjusted his bow tie and twirled the ends of his false moustache. "Let's hope for a quiet night," he muttered to himself as he closed the cave door. Inside, *Monsieur* Norbett ze bear, famous French chef, was polishing his pots and pans and humming to himself. He was dressed fully in his chef's outfit, complete with waxed moustache stuck firmly in place.

KNOCK! KNOCK! KNOCK! Someone was at the cave door. Norbett and Bamber exchanged glances.

KNOCK! KNOCK! KNOCK! went the door again and it was slowly pushed open. There, on the doorstep, stood the two kangaroos, Hoppy and Scuttle.

Norbett bustled forward, his French accent at the ready. *"Bonjour messieurs* kangaroos," he boomed, "a very big welcome to *Norbett's Bistro*, ze most famous and posh French restaurant in ze world."

Hoppy and Scuttle blinked and looked at one another in astonishment. Bamber glided into view, twirling his moustache and smiling as hard as he felt a posh head waiter in a very posh French restaurant would smile. Hoppy and Scuttle looked at him and their mouths dropped open.

"'Allo, 'allo," said Bamber, pulling the door open wider. He reached into his pocket and produced a white cloth which he draped over his left arm. "Come in, *messieurs*, come in. You look like very hungry kangaroos. 'Ave you come very far?"

Hoppy and Scuttle again exchanged astonished glances. Finally Hoppy cleared his throat and spoke. "We're looking for Dr Norbett Bear . . . " He stopped in mid-sentence and stared long and hard at Norbett. Norbett stood with a stupid smile fixed on his face, twirling the ends of his false moustache.

"You look just like Dr Norbett Bear," continued Hoppy, his eyes narrowing suspiciously.

"Mais oui," interrupted Norbett with a shrug of his shoulders and a twirl of his moustache, "everyone has made ze same mistake zis very day. I am Dr Norbett Bear's twin brother from France."

"FROM FRANCE!" chorused Hoppy and Scuttle together.

"Exactement, mon petits kangaroos. From France, in ze Serengeti region right beside . . . "

"Wexford," piped in Bamber, with a nod of his head and a twirl of his moustache for effect.

Hoppy and Scuttle exchanged worried glances.

"And where have you, *messieurs* ze kangaroos, come from?" asked Bamber.

"From Sydney, Australia," piped up Hoppy at last, trying hard to make sense of the visions in front of him.

Bamber put on his Puzzled Looking Face. "Sydney Australia? Never 'eard of him. He is not from around zese parts anyway."

Hoppy started to explain but decided better of it and shut up. He eyed Norbett and Bamber suspiciously again. "We've come to see the doctor," he said at last.

Scuttle nodded in agreement. He held up the pogo stick. "We wanted to return this," he added.

"Quel dommage," said Bamber, "what a pity. Ze famous Dr Norbett Bear and his faithful first assistant, the petit Bamber Bear, have just gone out."

"Who are you guys, then?" asked Hoppy.

"I am Bamber ze bear, ze head waiter in zis posh French restaurant," said Bamber grandly. He turned and placed his paw on Norbett's shoulder. "Zis is Norbett ze bear, ze one and only bear chef in ze whole wide world. He will cook such dishes that you will never before 'ave tasted in your kangarooish lives."

"Strewth, I could sure do with a bit of tucker," sighed Hoppy wearily, "it's been a long old day and a bit of decent food would sure go down a treat. What do you say, Scuttle?"

"No worries, mate," said Scuttle, halfway into the cave already. "I could eat an elephant, I'm so hungry."

"You may have to," muttered Bamber under his breath, remembering what little there was left in Norbett's larder. "Do sit down while I get ze menu," he said out loud and Hoppy and Scuttle hopped over to the table and sat down expectantly.

Norbett went to the back of the cave and started banging a few pots and pans together again. Bamber shuffled over beside him and whispered into his ear.

"What'll I offer them to eat? Where's the menu?"

Norbett held up a paw. He lifted an extra large pot up and from under it produced the first menu of *Norbett's Bistro,* a masterpiece he had been working on all the previous day.

"Oh, nice one," muttered Bamber as he read. "Nice one," he added when he had finished, not daring to mention to Norbett that he had eaten nearly everything that was written on it! He gave Norbett a rather weak smile and returned to the table, cloth draped over his left arm for effect. He lit a candle in the centre of the table, brushed a few imaginary crumbs away and handed the menu to the kangaroos who studied it hungrily.

"We 'ave ze mutton done in ze breadcrumbs, lightly cooked in ze charcoal oven and covered in ze chef's own special garlic sauce," began Bamber, reading for the kangaroos' benefit.

"Mmmm," went Hoppy and Scuttle together.

"Then we 'ave Norbett's Special French

Stew, served with ze freshly cut *pommes de terres.*"

"Mmmm," went Hoppy and Scuttle again, and Scuttle licked his lips.

"Then we 'ave Norbett's Special Catch of Ze Day, fresh fish from ze sea, lightly breaded and cooked to perfection with fresh herbs."

"Mmmmm . . . mmmm . . . mmmm," went Hoppy and Scuttle together, winking at each other in delight. "We're starving!"

"Then we 'ave beautiful dry toast," added Bamber finally.

"Toast?" exclaimed Hoppy and Scuttle. "TOAST?"

"*Exactement, messieurs,* toast. Ze raw bread cut into ze teeny weeny slices, put under ze grill and lightly browned to your liking." Bamber finished with a grand flourish, flicking his cloth across the length of the table again and laying it gently across his arm. "I would recommend ze toast, monsieurs," he added solemnly.

"No way," began Scuttle, licking his lips and rubbing his tummy. He reached inside his pouch and produced a handkerchief which he tucked under his chin.

"I haven't come all this way to eat toast. I'm going to have the mutton."

"Me too," added Hoppy emphatically.

"Certainement," murmured Bamber and he glided back to Norbett, who by now had inspected his larder and discovered the damage Bamber had done. There was a heated exchange between them before Bamber finally returned to the kangaroos.

"I am terribly sorry, *messieurs*," he announced, "but ze mutton is all gone. Finished. Totally sold out. May I suggest ze toast?" he added hopefully.

"No!" chorused Hoppy and Scuttle together. "We'll have the Special French Stew."

"Certainement," murmured Bamber again, tugging at his bow tie nervously.

He glided back to Norbett who was waiting for him, a furious look on his face.

"You've gone and eaten almost every scrap of food I had stocked up in my larder," he hissed. Bamber shrugged his shoulders in a grand French gesture and pretended to blow his nose.

"And don't blow your nose on your apron!" Norbett snapped.

Bamber smiled weakly back.

"Now go and tell them we are completely out of the Special French Stew as well."

So Bamber straightened his bow tie and moved towards the table, humming nervously. Hoppy and Scuttle looked up expectantly, both licking their lips hungrily. Bamber smiled weakly at them.

"*Pardonnez-moi, messieurs,*" he announced solemnly "I am so sorry for you two kangaroos."

"Why?" chorused Hoppy and Scuttle.

"Because, *messieurs* ze kangaroos, ze famous chef in zis famous and posh-type restaurant has just informed me zat we are totally out of ze Norbett's Special French Stew."

Hoppy and Scuttle groaned.

"May I suggest ze toast?" Bamber added hopefully.

"No!" roared the kangaroos. "We're starving. We want some proper tucker, not just some Mickey Mouse slices of toast!"

"Ze toast has nothing to do with zis mouse called Mickey about whom you speak," sniffed Bamber. "It is ze house speciality. Raw bread, cut into ze teeny weeny slices, placed under ze grill and lightly browned to perfection." He smiled at the kangaroos and produced a pencil from his pocket and licked the end. "Now can I take your order for ze toast, *s'il vous plaît?*"

"No!" roared Hoppy and Scuttle together. "We don't want toast. We want some decent tucker!" They glanced again at the menu. "We want the Catch of the Day," Scuttle announced.

"Certainement," murmured Bamber. He

scribbled the order on a piece of paper. "*Certainement.*" He returned to Norbett.

Hoppy and Scuttle were now so hungry, they could hear their tummies rumbling. They looked on anxiously at Norbett and Bamber, heads together at the back of the cave. Every now and then Bamber ze bear, head waiter, threw an anxious glance in their direction. *Monsieur* Norbett ze bear, posh chef, seemed flustered, banging his pots and pans against one another. Finally Bamber came back to the table. He smiled nervously at the kangaroos who, by now, were so hungry they had started to nibble at the flowers in the centre of the table. They watched him approach, half dreading what they might hear.

"*Bonjour, messieurs* ze kangaroos, and a jolly good day to you both. Isn't it a beautiful evening out tonight? I do hope ze good weather will keep up for ze weekend, *n'est-ce pas*?"

Hoppy and Scuttle said nothing. They

just sat, open-mouthed, waiting to hear the worst.

"I am afraid," continued Bamber solemnly, "zat Norbett's Special Catch of Ze Day ees off. Ze 'orrible leetle fishes refused to become ze Catch of Ze Day, and maybe if I cast my line tomorrow zey will become ze Catch of Tomorrow. Heh, heh. What do you think of my leetle joke? Heh, heh – ze Catch of Tomorrow!"

"Oh, No!" groaned Hoppy and Scuttle out loud. "We're starving and you've nothing to eat in this dump. What sort of a restaurant is this with no food in it?" They were becoming quite angry by now.

Bamber held up a paw for silence. He put on his I'm In Charge Here face.

"There is still ze toast. Ze raw bread, cut into ze teeny weeny slices, lightly browned under ze grill, served with ze lashings of butter."

By this stage Hoppy and Scuttle were so hungry and tormented they would have eaten the legs off the table. Their stomachs were rumbling like thunder and they were drooling at the thought of food, any food, just some sort of food!

"YES PLEASE!" they chorused. "OH, YES PLEASE. GIVE US THE TOAST! JUST GIVE US SOMETHING TO EAT!"

"Certainement," murmured Bamber, "and if I may say so, zis is an excellent choice."

Within minutes *Monsieur* Norbett ze bear, head chef in the posh and famous *Norbett's Bistro*, had produced plate upon plate of hot buttery toast and the kangaroos devoured it, slice after slice after slice. Only Scuttle's portions were liberally smeared with Mexican jumping beans, enough to put the hop back into any hopless kangaroo.

"Mmmm," they raved as fresh portions were laid on the table. "Mmmmm . . . mmmm . . . mmmm . . . what lovely toast!"

Norbett and Bamber looked on with satisfied smiles, shrugging their shoulders

like good French chefs and head waiters do, any time the kangaroos looked up. "An excellent choice, *messieurs* ze kangaroos, an excellent choice indeed," murmured Bamber as he cleared the table and flicked the last crumb away. He blew out the candle as the kangaroos got up to leave.

"Strewth, that was some tucker we had there, *Monsieur* Norbett ze bear," said Hoppy as he opened the cave door. "That's what I call real French cooking!"

Norbett brushed these words away with a wave of his paw and murmured something French like "Eiffel Tower."

Outside in the night air Hoppy and Scuttle rubbed their full bellies and hopped off into the forest in the general direction of Australia. Scuttle, in particular, seemed to be able to take large and extremely strong leaps into the air. Hoppy looked on in amazement.

"See ya later, bears," Hoppy shouted back. "Ya can tell Dr Norbett Bear that Scuttle has learned how to hop again. He'll be real pleased."

Bamber kept waving until he saw them finally disappear behind some trees.

He turned to go back into the cave just

in time to see Norbett Bear charge at him with the biggest pot in the kitchen.

"Help!" growled Bamber as he took to his heels through the forest and the safety of his cave, hotly pursued by Norbett. "You're supposed to be the head waiter, not my best customer!" roared Norbett. "You've eaten my reastaurant out in one fell swoop!"

Bamber didn't stop to answer, he just kept running.

6

Mr Dog the Windbag

The next day Bamber Bear, faithful first assistant to Dr Norbett Bear MD, reported for duty as usual at the Forest Medical Centre. Norbett had been up and about earlier and had placed a new sign at the cave door. Bamber inspected it closely:

Norbett's Bistro
Grand Opening Tonight
Posh French Food Cooked to Perfection
Your Chef Tonight: Monsieur Norbett ze bear,
Famous French Chef
(Twin brother of ze famous Dr Norbett bear MD)
Your Head Waiter Tonight: Bamber ze bear,
ze Posh Head Waiter
(Twin brother of ze famous Bamber bear FA)
Book Now to Avoid Disappointment!

"Mmm, very nice," thought Bamber as he read. He was looking forward to showing off his new head waiter's uniform again.

Inside the cave Norbett was putting away all the food he could collect. His scowl warned Bamber away from the kitchen. Bamber made a Most Unpleasant Face at him from behind a paw.

"Bamber Bear," snapped Norbett, "are you pulling faces at me again?"

"Moi?" replied Bamber innocently, "little ol' *moi*, pulling faces? How could you believe such a thing possible?"

Norbett scowled again and turned to lock away some rare black olives before putting on his doctor's uniform. Bamber was already wearing his first assistant uniform.

"OK," said Norbett, admiring himself in the long mirror at the back of the cave, "show the first patient in. And don't forget," he added, "try and get as many customers as you can for our opening night tonight at the *bistro*." He flicked a few stray hairs away from his sleeve. "Oh, and I forgot to tell you, we have a very special guest coming."

"Special guest?" asked Bamber. "Special guest? You never said anything about a special guest. Who is this special guest?"

"Mr Egon Runnay," replied Norbett grandly, "the world-famous restaurant critic from the Outside World."

"From the Outside World!" Bamber gasped in amazement. "Mr Egon Runnay! The world-famous restaurant critic!" he exclaimed. Then he paused and put on his Very Puzzled Looking Face. "Who's he?"

"He is a world-famous restaurant critic, Bamber *mon petit,*" replied Norbett grandly, "and he has heard of our *bistro.* He is coming tonight to watch us in action. If we can impress him he will award us a rosette and we will become just as famous for our cooking as we now are for our cures."

Bamber rubbed his paws together in glee.

"We will become the first bears to have successfully opened a posh French restaurant and to be Egon Runnay recommended," Norbett added.

"I like it! I like it!" squealed Bamber with delight. "Bamber ze bear, ze famous head waiter of *Norbett's Bistro*, will become an international star!"

"Exactement, mon petit," said Norbett, grinning from ear to ear. "But first we have to do some doctoring. Show in the first patient."

"*Oui, oui,* Dr ze bear. *Oui, oui,*" giggled Bamber as he threw open the cave door.

Into the cave struggled a rather mangey-looking dog. He was scratching himself and blowing his nose and moaning and groaning and generally looking miserable. He sat on his hind legs at the table in front of Norbett.

"What's the matter with you, Mr Dog?" asked Norbett.

The dog sneezed and scratched at his backside and then picked at his nose.

Bamber and Norbett exchanged glances and put on their We're Disgusted With All This Faces. The dog produced a rather tatty piece of paper and began his litany of woe.

"It's me hind legs, doctor," he started. "They just don't seem to want to keep up with me front legs. They're an awful nuisance. I can hardly chase any oul' flea-bitten cats any more for me hind legs. Me front legs do what they're supposed to do, they run at the front. But me hind legs just lag behind as if they couldn't be bothered with the rest of me at all and I'm rightly fed up trying to pull them after me."

Norbett opened his mouth to say something but the dog was off again with another item on his list. "Now there's another thing I'd like you to look at while I'm here. Do you see that front paw?" Here he thrust a rather muddy paw into Norbett's face. "Do you see that paw? That paw has me heart broke. That paw will be the death of me. That paw, that paw I'm showing you right now, that paw I'd trade in for a new paw any day of the week. Which is sad really, for me and that paw have been great mates for years."

He paused and gave a little groan. Norbett's face was getting longer with every minute. Bamber tried hard not to smirk.

"In fact," moaned the dog, "I never had a better right paw – up until recently, that is."

"What's the matt . . . " Norbett tried to interrupt but the dog was off again.

"That right paw gives me gip, so it does. If it's not itching me, it's hurting me, and if it's not hurting me, it's scalding me. And if it's not scalding me, it's freezing me. I'd like you to do something about that right paw."

Norbett tried to open his mouth again but the dog was in full flight and would not be stopped. He snarled at Norbett. "Do you see those teeth?" he asked "They used to be great teeth altogether. I couldn't tell you how many bones I've chewed with those teeth. I couldn't tell you how many sausages I've eaten with those teeth. I just couldn't tell you how many cats' backsides I've snapped at with those teeth. Those were great teeth. But do you see them now?" He bared them again for Norbett.

"I do," said Norbett wearily.

"Well they're neither use nor ornament to me now. Those teeth have had their day. Those teeth will chew neither bones nor sausages any more. Those teeth," he ended at last, "have been put into retirement."

"Right," growled Norbett, seizing his chance now that the dog had paused. "I'll get my faithful first assistant to make up some special medicines for all those problems."

"Good bear yourself," said the dog. "But," he added quickly, "there's more. I haven't finished yet."

"I just knew you hadn't," muttered Bamber under his breath.

"I was wondering," continued the dog, "can you do anything for a runny nose? I suffer terribly from a runny nose. I can't do any decent sniffing about the place without me nose letting me down. I'm just picking up the trail of a rat or a cat or a nice juicy bone and, before you know it, me nose starts to sneeze and run and I've lost the trail altogether."

"I would . . . " Norbett tried unsuccessfully to butt in again.

"Then there's me dandruff." The dog

was off again. He started to scratch at his head. "I'm tormented with dandruff. I can't ask any girlfriends out to join me for a bit of cat chasing, or to chew over an oul' bone, but that they're not commenting about me dandruff. I'm just covered in white stuff, all over me good coat. Or what used to be a good coat. I'm coming to that next . . ."

Bamber and Norbett groaned together.

"That coat, me hairy covering, the stuff that keeps the cold off me in winter: well, it's had it. It's looking mangey and flea-bitten and tatty." He scratched his neck vigorously with a front paw. "Now I used to be real proud of me coat, all glossy and shiny it was like you see on other dogs who eat Winalot and get to go to London and win the Crufts dog show. But that self-same coat has become a nightmare. I've had more fleas hanging out of me than enough."

Norbett started to feel itchy and moved further away from the dog. Bamber moved right out of the cave altogether.

"In fact," continued the dog, enjoying the bit of attention he was getting, "even the fleas have taken to moving out of me coat. So many of their friends and neighbours have had such a good time nesting in my coat that there's nothing left for them to enjoy any more. Me nice shiny, Winalot-look coat looks more like an oul' tatty blanket. Just like me teeth, me coat has had it s day. Into the rubbish bin it would go only that means I'd have to go in with it." He gave a little laugh. "Bad and all as it is I'm still very attached to it. Heh, heh, heh. I'm still very attached to me oul coat! Heh, heh, heh." The dog couldn't stop himself now and began an irritating laugh that nearly drove Norbett mad. He put both paws over his ears and looked around for Bamber who was nowhere to be seen.

The dog was still chuckling at his joke when the cave door slowly creaked open and a loud "Miaaooww" came from outside. His ears pricked up and he stopped chuckling.

"Miaooww," came again from just outside the cave door.

Norbett looked at the door, puzzled. The dog's ears flickered and he stood up suddenly.

"Miaoow, miaoow, miaoow."

The dog slunk down on all fours and slithered towards the door. A low rumbling growl formed in the back of his throat.

"Go on, scram, you thieving cat!" came a roar from outside and suddenly Bamber burst in through the front door looking very agitated. "Quick!" he shouted, "somebody, quick! A big fat cat has gone and stolen one of our best and juiciest bones from the kitchen. He's just escaped into the forest with it!"

Norbett jumped to his feet and started towards the door. Before he could get anywhere near it the dog gave an almighty

roar and leapt outside into the clearing, barking and growling with all his might. He took off like greased lightning in the general direction of the forest, barking and growling and snapping for all he was worth. He looked like a champion sprinter. Norbett was just about to follow when Bamber grabbed him by the tail of his doctor's coat. "It's OK," he hissed loudly. "It was only me. I couldn't think of any other way to get rid of that old windbag."

Norbett looked at Bamber in surprise. Then he started laughing . . . and laughing

. . . and laughing. Before long Bamber joined in, and the two had to sit down at the table for support. Bamber was holding his sides and Norbett kept wiping away tears of laughter.

"His hind legs don't seem to be lagging behind him right now!" giggled Bamber.

"No," chortled Norbett, "and those teeth looked fairly strong to me from where I could see them!"

Bamber put up a paw for silence. "By the way, we're booked out for tonight," he announced.

"What!" exclaimed Norbett.

"While you and Mr Dog were having such a long and detailed chat," explained Bamber, "I slipped outside to see how I could get rid of him. Lo and behold, while I was standing there three different groups of the forest animals came along and booked themselves in for tonight's grand opening."

Norbett rubbed his paws together in delight. "Great work, Bamber Bear, my faithful first assistant. Absolutely great work. Now let's shut up shop here and get some rest before tonight." He slipped out of his doctor's coat. "Don't forget," he added, "we have to make a big impression on Mr Egon Runnay."

"Do not worry your leetle bear-type head," said Bamber. "'e will have a night 'e will never forget."

"Attaboy, Bamber," cheered Norbett, "attaboy."

7

Chaos at the *Bistro*!

Bamber Bear stood admiring himself in front of the long mirror at the back of Norbett's cave. He was fully dressed in his head waiter's outfit and looked a picture. Beside him stood Norbett Bear, wearing his chef's outfit. Bamber inspected one side, then the other and growled his satisfaction. He was very pleased with himself. Norbett solemnly handed him his false moustache and Bamber slowly and deliberately fixed it to his top lip and stood back to admire the final result.

"You look a very handsome bear," said Norbett.

Bamber pulled in his stomach and nodded. "'Allo, Bamber ze bear, ze very famous head waiter in ze very famous and posh *Norbett's Bistro,*" he said to his reflection. He pressed his moustache down firmly again and turned to Norbett. "OK, *monsieur* Norbett ze bear, ze very famous chef of *Norbett's Bistro*, let us open ze doors. Let ze evening begin!"

"Ouvrez la porte," corrected Norbett. "You mean, *'ouvrez la porte'*, Bamber *mon petit."*

"Exactement," agreed Bamber, *"ouvrez la porte*. But first we must open ze door."

Norbett started to say something but thought the better of it. *"Exactement,* Bamber *mon petit, exactement."*

Norbett went to the back of the cave and waited. Bamber went to the front of the cave, placed a paw on the door handle, paused and then nodded towards Norbett. *Monsieur* Norbett ze bear, ze very famous and posh chef in ze very famous and posh

Norbett's Bistro, nodded back. *"Ouvrez la porte,"* he whispered. "I will after I've opened the door," Bamber whispered back. He turned and pulled the cave door open with a grand and dramatic Gallic flourish. *"Bonsoir, messieurs et mesdames,"* he announced loudly, "welcome to ze grand opening night of *Norbett's Bistro*, ze most famous and most posh French restaurant in all ze world!"

He looked down and there, waiting, were two goats, two pigs and two horses.

"Aha! *Monsieur* and *Madame* Goats! *Quel surprise!* What a delight to 'ave you 'ere tonight. Do come in."

The goats looked at Bamber and then looked at one another before sprightly jumping inside the cave and rushing to one of the tables.

"And *Monsieur* and *Madame* Oink ze pigs! You are looking so well! Ah, *Madame* Oink, is that French perfume I smell on you?"

"Oink!" went Madame Oink. "Oink! No, it's not French perfume, it's fresh swill."

"But ze very special swill, all ze same," beamed Bamber. He turned to hold his nose as Monsieur and Madame Oink shuffled inside.

"*Monsieur* Gallop, ze horse. I am so ze delighted that you and *Madame* Gallop could join us tonight. Do come in."

The horses neighed in reply and clip-clopped over to their tables. Bamber was just about to close the door when through the clearing rushed a figure, clutching a piece of paper.

"Excuse me," came a very posh voice, "I'm looking for *Norbett's Bistro*."

"So is everyone," said Bamber, inspecting the man now standing on the doorstep. "But we are full up for ze evening."

"I'm Egon Runnay. I've travelled an awfully long way to be here tonight. I've come to report on this restaurant and see if it should be in my world-famous guide."

"Aha, *Monsieur* Egon Runnay," beamed Bamber, "you are most welcome. We 'ave reserved a special table for you near ze window."

So into *Norbett's Bistro* went Egon Runnay, the world-famous restaurant critic, all the time inspecting and noting everything around him.

Norbett came out from the kitchen banging his pots and pans together as usual. He cleared his throat and held up a blackboard with the evening's menu written on it. *"Bonsoir, Messieurs et Mesdames,"* he shouted over the noisy babble at the tables. "Welcome to *Norbett's Bistro*. Do 'ave a look at tonight's special opening menu especially created for you. My head waiter, Bamber ze bear, will take your orders in a moment."

Bamber smiled and nodded.

The goats, the pigs, the horses and Mr Egon Runnay inspected the menu closely. Bamber waited for a moment before presenting himself at the table where Monsieur and Madame Gallop the horses sat. He pulled out a pencil stub from behind his ear and licked the end of it.

"Are we ready to place ze order? What would *Monsieur* Gallop like?"

"Hay," said *Monsieur* Gallop.

Bamber looked at him, puzzled, his pencil poised over his order book.

"Heh?"

"Yes. Hay."

"Heh?" said Bamber again. "Heh what?"

"Hay! Hay!" snapped monsieur Gallop. "Hay! Hay! Hay! Hay!"

Bamber looked at the horse pitifully. "Hay, hay, hay! to you too, *Monsieur* Gallop ze horse. But what would you like to eat?"

"HAY!" roared the horse and Bamber flinched. The other animals looked up suddenly. Mr Egon Runnay scribbled something in his notebook.

"HAY!" roared the horse again, "I want some hay to eat!"

"Oh, hay!" gasped Bamber in relief, "you want to eat hay?"

"Exactly," snapped the horse. "Now get on with it, bear. We're starving."

Bamber murmured something, returned to Norbett and broke the news.

Mr Egon Runnay watched their every move. Norbett listened carefully, one eye on Mr Egon Runnay to see how he was taking all this. He whispered something back and Bamber moved on to the pigs. "Are we ready to order, *Monsieur* and *Madame* Oink?"

"Slops," muttered *Monsieur* Oink from behind a trotter. "Have you any decent slops to eat? Me and Mrs Oink don't much fancy all this fancy food. We'd much prefer a few buckets of slops. You know, lots of leftovers, preferably a few days old and we could wash it all down with some sour milk."

Bamber looked as if he would get sick and placed one paw across his mouth, the other over his tummy for support. He began to feel a bit hot under the collar and he loosened his bow tie with a claw.

He put his head down closer to *Monsieur* Oink's right ear and murmured into it. "*Monsieur* Oink, zis is a posh French restaurant 'ere. We serve only ze best and poshest of freshly-prepared food. Zis is not ze tiphead for ze mangey animals!"

Monsieur Oink started to say something but Bamber was already back beside Norbett in the kitchen. Norbett's eyes rolled in his head as he listened to the latest news from the restaurant floor. He bared his teeth and banged two large pots together angrily. From his window seat Mr Egon Runnay looked up, startled, before scribbling something else in his notebook. Norbett watched this anxiously and murmured to Bamber who nodded in agreement. Bamber put on a real wide smile and oiled his way over to Mr Egon Runnay. "Ah, *Monsieur* Egon Runnay, a big *bonne nuit* to you and all of your family and ze friends. What would you like to order from our special opening menu?"

Mr Egon Runnay smiled back at Bamber. "I would like to order some Norbett's Special Fish Platter and a little of Norbett's Freshly Prepared Stew and a little also of Norbett's Vegetarian Pie. Could I also have some of Norbett's Home-Made Ice Cream, Norbett's Apple Pie, and Norbett's French Gâteau? This chef certainly seems to be a very busy bear-making all these dishes himself."

Bamber's mouth dropped. "You want to eat them all?"

"No," said Mr Egon Runnay, "I most certainly *do not* want to eat them all but I wish to *taste* them all."

Bamber could feel his knees getting weak and he leaned heavily against the table. He looked over at Norbett, who was watching this exchange anxiously.

Bamber gave him a weak smile, and slowly made his way back towards the kitchen and passed on the bad news.

Norbett looked as if he would blow his top. "He doesn't want to eat all this food, he only wants to taste it!" he growled, chewing on his apron to stifle his voice. Bamber nodded glumly.

"BEAR!" came a roar from one of the tables, interrupting them. "BEAR!"

Norbett and Bamber looked over quickly. Monsieur Goat was standing up on his chair on his hind legs. Madame Goat was staring hard at Bamber, pointing towards her mouth with a front hoof.

"WE WANT SOMETHING TO EAT!" they shouted together. "HOW ABOUT SOME SERVICE HERE?"

Mr Egon Runnay noted all this down.

Norbett gave Bamber a nudge. "I'll pile up Mr Egon Runnay's plate. You go and sort out those two goats before they cause any trouble."

So Bamber rushed over to the goats' table, a forced smile on his face. He twirled at the ends of his false moustache and straightened his bow tie. "*Bonne nuit* again, *Monsieur* and *Madame* ze goats, and may I say, madame how absolutely radiant you look tonight. Have you had your beard brushed just for this evening?" Madame Goat blushed and hid her head behind a hoof.

"I WANT TO ORDER SOMETHING TO EAT!" snapped *Monsieur* Goat loudly. "MY WIFE AND I ARE STARVING. WHAT DO YOU HAVE TO DO TO GET SOME SERVICE IN THIS DUMP?"

Mr Egon Runnay scribbled his observations down, watching Bamber carefully. Norbett held his breath as he piled up Mr Egon Runnay's plate. Bamber fixed *Monsieur* ze goat with a look that would kill. He opened his mouth to say something but the goat was off again, whinnying at his loudest.

"WE'RE STARVING! WE COULD EAT A HORSE!"

Bamber clamped a paw over *Monsieur* ze goat's mouth before he could say any more. But it was too late. From the next table, *Monsieur* Gallop ze horse stood up slowly and turned towards *Monsieur* ze goat. "What was that you're just after saying there, goat? Did you say you could eat a horse?" He reared up on his hind legs. "Just try saying that again, this time to my face."

Bamber tried to interrupt. "Pleeze, *Monsieur* ze Gallop, no fighting in zis very posh French restaurant. I am sure that *Monsieur* ze goat was only joking, weren't you *Monsieur*?" he clamped his paws tighter around the goat's mouth. Monsieur Nanny ze goat struggled to free himself, finally prising Bamber's paws away. He let out a roar.

"TAKE YOUR PAWS OFF ME, BEAR! WHAT KIND OF A DUMP IS THIS? THIS PLACE ISN'T EVEN FIT FOR A PIG TO EAT IN!"

Bamber held his head in both paws and groaned. From a side table *Monsieur* and *Madame* Oink ze pigs slowly stood up and made their way to the table where *Monsieur* ze goat and his wife, *Madame*, were protesting. "What's that you said there, goat, about this place not being fit for a pig to eat in?" snuffled *Monsieur* Oink angrily. He raised a trotter and poked *Monsieur* Goat in the eye. "You've insulted me and my wife, Mrs Oink, and you had better say you're sorry or you're going to get a lot more than a poke in the eye from a trotter."

"Hear, hear," agreed *Monsieur* Gallop and he brought his front hoof down heavily on *Monsieur* Goat's head.

"Keep out of this, horse," snapped *Monsieur* Oink, "this is a private argument between me and this bearded wonder. No goat insults me and my lovely wife, Mrs Oink, and gets away with it."

"I want a go at him first," snapped *Monsieur* Gallop, reaching across to grab *Monsieur* Goat's beard. *Monsieur* Oink caught a hold of his foreleg and held on tight. "He's mine," he snuffled angrily and pushed *Monsieur* Gallop back against the table. Bamber tried to stop *Monsieur* Gallop falling but it was too late. The table slid in front of him and he crashed to the ground. *Madame* Gallop jumped up and bashed *Monsieur* Oink across his snout, causing him to slither across the restaurant floor, dragging *Monsieur* Goat along with him by the beard. Madame Nanny Goat let out an angry roar as she watched her beloved husband land in a heap against the far wall. She jumped nimbly on to the table and bit *Monsieur* Oink on the ear and he let out a squeal of pain. Madame Oink leapt across and pushed the table over as *Madame* Goat's hoofs skidded furiously on the surface. Within seconds she too was lying in a heap on the floor.

Bamber was still holding on to *Monsieur* Gallop, trying desperately to restrain him as he clambered angrily to his feet, looking for *Monsieur* Oink. Just as he got onto all four legs, madame Oink slid across the floor and carried the legs from under him again. CRASH! *Monsieur* Gallop was lying on the flat of his back again, like a beached whale, all four legs waving furiously in the air.

Just at this point, unfortunately, monsieur Norbett ze bear, ze very famous and posh chef in ze very famous and posh French restaurant known as *Norbett's Bistro,* started across the skating rink that had become the restaurant floor. Held carefully in both paws and balancing precariously was a plate full of Norbett's Special Fish Platter, Norbett's Freshly Prepared Stew, Norbett's Vegetarian Pie, Norbett's Home-Made Ice Cream, Norbett's Apple Pie and Norbett's French Gâteau. All on one plate and all for Mr Egon Runnay, the world-famous restaurant critic, the one man capable of awarding a rosette to *Norbett's Bistro* and making it world-famous.

At that precise moment Mr Egon Runnay was standing on top of his table, scribbling away furiously in his notebook as he watched the developing chaos. *Monsieur* Oink was wrestling with *Monsieur*

Within seconds they were all lying in a heap on the floor

Goat and dragging him by the beard across the floor. *Madame* Oink and *Monsieur* Gallop were tripping each other up at the far corner, knocking over the few tables and chairs still standing. *Madame* Gallop and *Madame* Goat were exchanging insults and trying to get a good swipe at one another. Norbett stepped over *Monsieur* Oink, skipped over *Monsieur* Goat but failed to negotiate the body of Bamber Bear, now lying in a heap on the floor, having himself fallen as he had tried to separate the combatants.

"AAAGGGHHH!" went Norbett as he caught his toe on Bamber's backside. Out from his paws and into the air flew the plate piled high with Mr Egon Runnay's order.

"AAAGGHH!" screamed Mr Egon Runnay watching helplessly as the plate and its contents spun round and round across the restaurant, straight towards him.

SPLAT! Into the face of Mr Egon Runnay, the world-famous restaurant critic and awarder of rosettes, went Norbett's Freshly Fish Platter, Norbett's Specially Prepared Stew, Norbett's Vegetarian Pie, Norbett's Home-Made Ice Cream, Norbett's Apple Pie, and last but very much not least, Norbett's French Gâteau. SPLAT! SPLAT! SLITHER, SLITHER! SQUELCH! The food all merged into one enormous blob covering his face, trickling down his nose, and on to his precious notebook.

"Egad!" went Mr Egon Runnay, before slipping on the wet floor and sliding on to the ground.

When the food hit the floor the two bears, the two pigs, the two goats, the two horses and Mr Egon Runnay started sliding all over the place, trying desperately to regain their footing. As *Monsieur* Oink slipped and slithered he kept swiping at *Monsieur* Goat, who in turn threw a few stray punches at *Monsieur* Gallop, succeeding only in clipping Norbett, ze very famous and posh chef, across the ear. Norbett howled in pain.

Bamber, ze head waiter in *Norbett's Bistro*, stumbled directly into Mr Egon Runnay as he tried to retrieve his precious notebook, his face still covered in a combination of ice cream, fish, vegetarian pie and French gâteau.

Down in a heap he plopped again. "OUCH!" he winced, as his bottom hit the edge of an upturned chair.

In the midst of all this confusion and mayhem, Norbett's waxed moustache began to peel away from his upper lip and his chef's hat was knocked off his head. Within minutes his chef's outfit lay torn and tattered at his feet and he stood in the middle of the restaurant, covered in his own food, nursing a sore ear, dressed only in his trousers which were held up by his famous red braces.

"THAT'S NOT *MONSIEUR* NORBETT ZE BEAR, ZE VERY FAMOUS FRENCH CHEF. THAT'S NORBETT BEAR, THE *REAL* NORBETT BEAR WHO LIVES HERE!" came a surprised roar from *Madame* Gallop. The goats stopped fighting with the pigs and the pigs stopped punching at the horses and Mr Egon Runnay peered from behind a generous dollop of Norbett's Home-Made Ice Cream to find Norbett looking like the cat who was caught stealing the cream.

BANG! BOING! BANG! BOING! BANG!

BOING! From the back of the kitchen leapt Bamber Bear, crashing two of Norbett's largest pans against one another. "FIRE! FIRE! FIRE!" he roared at the top of his voice. "CLEAR THE *BISTRO*! CLEAR THE *BISTRO*! FIRE! FIRE!" BANG! BOING! BANG! BOING! went the pans again. "CLEAR THE *BISTRO*! FIRE! FIRE!"

"RUN!" screamed *Madame* Oink, and never as fast before in his pig-type life did *Monsieur* Oink get to his trotters and disappear out the cave door. He was followed just as quickly by monsieur and *Madame* Goat and *Monsieur* and *Madame* Gallop. Taking up the rear was that world-famous restaurant critic and awarder of rosettes, Mr Egon Runnay, clutching his equally famous, but now heavily stained, notebook.

"Did we win a rosette?" roared Bamber after him as he disappeared through the clearing and into the safety of the bushes. He turned round to find Norbett wiping a layer of French gâteau off his face. "He didn't say whether we won a rosette," complained Bamber.

Norbett blew a layer of cream away from his upper lip and licked some pastry off his chin. He looked at Bamber and Bamber looked back. For a few moments they said nothing. Then Norbett began to giggle. "Did we win a rosette?" he sniggered, "did we win a rosette? Ha, ha, ha. Did we win a rosette? Bamber Bear, it's not a posh French restaurant we should run here. This should be called Norbett's boxing ring!" He held his sides and laughed the loudest belly-laugh Bamber had ever heard him laugh before. "Forget about *Norbett's Bistro*, from now on this place will hold world championship boxing fights. Ha, ha, ha . . . aagghh!" CRASH! Norbett tumbled to the ground as he slipped on a slice of his home-made apple pie.

Bamber twirled his waxed moustache

and straightened his bow tie. He pulled his head waiter's coat together at the front. "*Au revoir, Monsieur* Norbett bear, ze famous French chef. I will now return to my own cave for a rest."

"Don't forget to 'ferme la porte' after you," shouted Norbett.

"I will after I've closed the door," said Bamber.

8

The End

Bamber Bear inspected the sign outside Norbett Bear's cave the next morning:

NORBETT'S BISTRO
SPECIAL ANNOUNCEMENT
THE *BISTRO* IS NOW CLOSED
PERMANENTLY
(If the animals in this forest don't know how to behave themselves then they shouldn't expect classy restaurants!)

"Nice one, Norbett," agreed Bamber, secretly disappointed to be losing out on wearing his special head waiter uniform.

Out from his cave strode Norbett bear, both paws behind his red braces which he snapped against his chest.

"Aha, Bamber Bear," he said grandly, "what do you think of my new sign?"

"I think you're right," said Bamber, looking at the sign again. "Anyway, I don't think I am ready for working nights as well as days."

"No, Bamber Bear," agreed Norbett, "maybe that *was* a bit much to ask. I think we will stick to what we do so well, healing the sick and infirm animals of the world. We're quite famous now, you know."

Bamber was about to say something when he noticed a movement in the bushes. He held up a paw for silence. Into the clearing slithered a fox, clutching an empty bottle in his front paws. He looked furtively this way and that before making a dash for the cave. "Dr Norbett Bear," he panted when he reached Norbett and Bamber.

"Yes, fox?" replied Norbett, "what can I do for you?"

"Memory medicine. I need some more memory medicine. My brain's addled and I can't think straight," said the fox, his eyes darting this way and that, as if looking for someone. "The last time I called here I met a couple of French goons who looked just like you and your faithful first assistant, Bamber Bear." Bamber and Norbett exchanged secret glances.

"They said they were your twin brothers from France. If you ask me they looked like Attila the Hun and his half-brother Attila the Bun!"

"Probably," interrupted Norbett, "however, they have gone back to France. The *bistro* has been closed for good."

"I'm not sorry to hear that," said the fox. "Those two were a real couple of loop-the-loops."

Bamber blew his nose to hide his grin. "Well, fox," he said, "I'll get you some more memory medicine right away." He disappeared inside the cave and returned with a fresh bottle of Norbett Bear's special memory medicine.

The fox read the label carefully. Then he read it again, a puzzled look on his face. He read it for the third time, shrugged his shoulders, and then placed the bottle carefully on the ground. He stood still on all four legs and then shook himself violently. He paused and then shook himself again. Norbett and Bamber's mouths dropped open. They stared at the fox as if he had two heads.

"What are you doing that for?" asked Bamber finally.

The fox picked up the bottle and inspected the label closely. "It says here: 'Shake well before taking this medicine'."

Bamber looked at Norbett and Norbett looked at Bamber. Then they both looked at the fox and shook their heads together sadly.

"Did I shake well enough, do you

think?" the fox asked anxiously. "Can I take my medicine now?"

"Yes, fox," sighed Bamber, "I've never seen a fox shake better in all my bear-type life."

The fox disappeared into the bushes, leaving Norbett and Bamber Bears still bemused.

Bamber turned to go inside the cave, when he noticed Norbett deep in thought. He groaned inwardly.

"Bamber Bear," said Norbett slowly.

Bamber groaned outwardly.

"I've just had another GREAT IDEA."

"Oh, no," groaned Bamber, outwardly and inwardly.

"Australia," said Norbett, a twinkle in his eyes again.

"Australia?" muttered Bamber.

"Yes, Australia," added Norbett. "I've been thinking about Australia."

Bamber Bear held his head in both paws, waiting for the next bit.

"I think," continued Norbett

enthusiastically, "I think we will go to Australia and sell pogo sticks to kangaroos!"

"AAAGGGHHH!" went Bamber Bear. "AAAGGGHHH!"

Deep in the forest the other animals heard Bamber's plaintive roars and ran to the safety of their lairs and burrows.

The next day Norbett and Bamber received a letter from the Outside World.

It was addressed to: *Messieurs* Norbett and Bamber Bears, c/o *Norbett's Bistro*. Norbett opened it slowly in front of Bamber. "It's from Mr Egon Runnay," he whispered and Bamber winced. Norbett read the contents out loud:

Dear Norbett and Bamber Bears,

Unfortunately I write to inform you that I have been unable to award you a rosette such that your restaurant might appear in my Guide to Posh French Restaurants.

However, I did enjoy my visit to your establishment a great deal. In fact, I haven't enjoyed myself so much in donkeys' years.

Perhaps you should reconsider a career in the restaurant business and think about opening a skating rink? Certainly I found that Norbett's Special Fish Platter when mixed with Norbett's Stew, Vegetarian Pie, Home-Made Ice Cream, Apple Pie and French Gâteau made for an excellent sliding surface.

Good luck for the future.

Mr Egon Runnay

Norbett looked at Bamber. "What do we think of that?" he asked.

"Pogo sticks!" they chorused together.

"Australia, here we come."

Also by Poolbeg

Norbett Bear, MD

By

Dr Paul Carson

FOREST MEDICAL CENTRE
PAINS EASED . . . SICKNESS CURED . . .
NO JOB TOO SMALL . . . COMMISSIONS TAKEN

When Dr Norbett Bear, MD and his faithful first assistant, Bamber Bear, FA, open the doors of the First Forest Medical Centre, anything can happen, and usually does!

"I think I've got German measles," announced the hare.
"Have you been to Germany?" snapped Norbett.
"No," replied the hare puzzled.
"Or received a postcard from Germany?"
"No."
"Or ever driven a Volkswagen?"
"What's a Volkswagen?" By now the hare was getting nervous.

The forest animals have never seen anything like Dr Norbett Bear before nor are they ever likely to want to again!

Read the hilarious exploits of Norbett and Bamber Bear, a visit to the doctor will never be the same again.

ISBN 1 85371 409 7 £3.99